IT COULD BE
Anything

IT COULD BE
Anything

KEITH LAUMER

ÆGYPAN PRESS

This text from *Amazing Stories,* January 1963.

Special thanks to Greg Weeks, Stephen Blundell, and the On-line Distributed Proofreading Team (which can be found at http://www.pgdp.net).

It Could Be Anything
A publication of
ÆGYPAN PRESS

www.aegypan.com

Keith Laumer, well-known for his tales of adventure and action, shows us a different side of his talent in this original, exciting and thought-provoking exploration of the meaning of meaning.

"She'll be pulling out in a minute, Brett," Mr. Phillips said. He tucked his railroader's watch back in his vest pocket. "You better get aboard — if you're still set on going."

"It was reading all them books done it," Aunt Haicey said. "Thick books, and no pictures in them. I knew it'd make trouble." She plucked at the faded hand-embroidered shawl over her thin shoulders, a tiny birdlike woman with bright anxious eyes.

"Don't worry about me," Brett said. "I'll be back."

"The place'll be yours when I'm gone," Aunt Haicey said. "Lord knows it won't be long."

"Why don't you change your mind and stay on, boy?" Mr. Phillips said, blinking up at the young man. "If I talk to Mr. J.D., I think he can find a job for you at the plant."

"So many young people leave Casperton," Aunt Haicey said. "They never come back."

Mr. Phillips clicked his teeth. "They write, at first," he said. "Then they gradually lose touch."

"All your people are here, Brett," Aunt Haicey said. "Haven't you been happy here?"

"Why can't you young folks be content with Casperton?" Mr. Phillips said. "There's everything you need here."

"It's that Pretty-Lee done it," Aunt Haicey said. "If it wasn't for that girl —"

A clatter ran down the line of cars. Brett kissed Aunt Haicey's dry cheek, shook Mr. Phillips' hand, and swung aboard. His suitcase was on one of the seats. He put it up above in the rack, and sat down, turned to wave back at the two old people.

It was a summer morning. Brett leaned back and watched the country slide by. It was nice country, Brett thought; mostly in corn, some cattle, and away in the distance the hazy blue hills. Now he would see what was on the other side of them: the cities, the mountains, and the ocean. Up until now all he knew about anything outside of Casperton was what he'd read or seen pictures of. As far as he was concerned, chopping wood and milking cows back in Casperton, they might as well not have existed. They were just words and pictures printed on paper. But he didn't want to just read about them. He wanted to see for himself.

*P*retty-Lee hadn't come to see him off. She was probably still mad about yesterday. She had been sitting at the counter at the Club Rexall, drinking a soda and reading a movie magazine with a big picture of an impossibly pretty face on the cover — the kind you never see just walking down the street. He had taken the next stool and ordered a coke.

"Why don't you read something good, instead of that pap?" he asked her.

"Something good? You mean something dry, I guess. And don't call it . . . that word. It doesn't sound polite."

"What does it say? That somebody named Doll Starr is fed up with glamour and longs for a simple home in the country and lots of kids? Then why doesn't she move to Casperton?"

"You wouldn't understand," said Pretty-Lee.

He took the magazine, leafed through it. "Look at this: all about people who give parties that cost thousands of dollars, and fly all over the world having affairs with each other and committing suicide and getting divorced. It's like reading about Martians."

"I still like to read about the stars. There's nothing wrong with it."

"Reading all that junk just makes you dissatisfied. You want to do your hair up crazy like the pictures in the magazines and wear weird-looking clothes —"

Pretty-Lee bent her straw double. She stood up and took her shopping bag. "I'm very glad to know you think my clothes are weird —"

"You're taking everything I say personally. Look." He showed her a full-color advertisement on the back cover of the magazine. "Look at this. Here's a man supposed to be cooking steaks on some kind of backyard grill. He looks like a movie star; he's dressed up like he was going to get married; there's not a wrinkle anywhere. There's not a spot on that apron. There isn't even a grease spot on the frying pan. The lawn is as smooth as a billiard table. There's his son; he looks just like his pop, except that he's not grey at the temples. Did you ever really see a man that handsome, or hair that was just silver over the ears and the rest glossy black? The daughter looks like a movie starlet, and her mom is exactly the same, except that she has that grey streak in front to match her husband. You can see the car in the drive; the treads of the tires must have just been scrubbed; they're not even dusty. There's not a pebble out of place; all the flowers are in full bloom; no dead ones. No leaves on the lawn; no dry twigs showing on the trees. That other house in the background looks like a palace, and the man with the rake, looking over the fence: he looks like this one's twin brother, and he's out raking leaves in brand new clothes —"

Pretty-Lee grabbed her magazine. "You just seem to hate everything that's nicer than this messy town —"

"I don't think it's nicer. I like you; your hair isn't always perfectly smooth, and you've got a mended place on your dress, and you feel human, you smell human —"

"Oh!" Pretty-Lee turned and flounced out of the drug store.

*B*rett shifted in the dusty plush seat and looked around. There were a few other people in the car. An old man was reading a newspaper; two old ladies whispered together. There was a woman of about thirty with a mean-looking kid; and some others. They didn't look like magazine pictures, any of them. He tried to picture them doing the things you read in newspapers: the old ladies putting poison in somebody's tea; the old man giving orders to start a war. He thought about babies in houses in cities, and airplanes flying over, and bombs falling down: huge explosive bombs. Blam! Buildings fall in, pieces of glass and stone fly through the air. The babies are blown up along with everything else —

But the kind of people he knew couldn't do anything like that. They liked to loaf and eat and talk and drink beer and buy a new tractor or refrigerator and go fishing. And if they ever got mad and hit somebody — afterwards they were embarrassed and wanted to shake hands. . . .

The train slowed, came to a shuddery stop. Through the window he saw a cardboardy-looking building with the words BAXTER'S JUNCTION painted across it. There were a few faded posters on a bulletin board. An old man was sitting on a bench, waiting. The two old ladies got off and a boy in blue jeans got on. The train started up. Brett folded his jacket and tucked it under his head and tried to doze off. . . .

*B*rett awoke, yawned, sat up. The train was slowing. He remembered you couldn't use the toilets while the train was stopped. He got up and went to the end of the car. The door was jammed. He got it open and went inside and closed the door behind him. The train was going slower, clack-clack . . . clack-clack . . . clack; clack . . . cuh-lack . . .

He washed his hands, then pulled at the door. It was stuck. He pulled harder. The handle was too small; it was hard to get hold of. The train came to a halt. Brett braced himself and strained against the door. It didn't budge.

He looked out the grimy window. The sun was getting lower. It was about three-thirty, he guessed. He couldn't see anything but some dry-looking fields.

Outside in the corridor there were footsteps. He started to call, but then didn't. It would be too embarrassing, pounding on the door and yelling, "Let me out! I'm stuck in the toilet . . ."

He tried to rattle the door. It didn't rattle. Somebody was dragging something heavy past the door. Mailbags, maybe. He'd better yell. But damnit, the door couldn't be all that hard to open. He studied the latch. All he had to do was turn it. He got a good grip and twisted. Nothing.

He heard the mailbag bump-bump, and then another one. To heck with it; he'd yell. He'd wait until he heard the footsteps pass the door again and then he'd make some noise.

Brett waited. It was quiet now. He rapped on the door anyway. No answer. Maybe there was nobody left in the car. In a minute the train would start up and he'd be stuck here until the next stop. He banged on the door. "Hey! The door is stuck!"

It sounded foolish. He listened. It was very quiet. He pounded again. The car creaked once. He put his ear to the door. He couldn't hear anything. He turned back to the window. There was no one in sight. He put his cheek flat against it, looked along the car. He saw only dry fields.

He turned around and gave the door a good kick. If he damaged it, it was too bad; the railroad shouldn't have defective locks on the doors. If they tried to make him pay for it, he'd tell them they were lucky he didn't sue the railroad . . .

*H*e braced himself against the opposite wall, drew his foot back, and kicked hard at the lock. Something broke. He pulled the door open.

He was looking out the open door and through the window beyond. There was no platform, just the same dry fields he could see on the other side. He came out and went along to his seat. The car was empty now.

He looked out the window. Why had the train stopped here? Maybe there was some kind of trouble with the engine. It had been sitting here for ten minutes or so now. Brett got up and went along to the door, stepped down onto the iron step. Leaning out, he could see the train stretching along ahead, one car, two cars —

There was no engine.

Maybe he was turned around. He looked the other way. There were three cars. No engine there either. He must be on some kind of siding . . .

Brett stepped back inside, and pushed through into the next car. It was empty. He walked along the length of it, into the next car. It was empty too. He went back through the two cars and his own car and on, all the way to the end of the train. All the cars were empty. He stood on the platform at the end of the last car, and looked back along the rails. They ran straight, through the dry fields, right to the horizon. He stepped down to the ground, went along the cindery bed to the front of the train, stepping on the ends of the wooden ties. The coupling stood open. The tall, dusty coach stood silently on its iron wheels, waiting. Ahead the tracks went on —

And stopped.

He walked along the ties, following the iron rails, shiny on top, and brown with rust on the sides. A hundred feet from the train they ended. The cinders went on another ten feet and petered out. Beyond, the fields closed in. Brett looked up at the sun. It was lower now in the west, its light getting yellow and late-afternoonish. He turned and looked back at the train. The cars stood high and prim, empty, silent. He walked back, climbed in, got his bag down from the rack, pulled on his jacket. He jumped down to the cinders, followed them to where they ended. He hesitated a moment, then pushed between the knee-high stalks. Eastward across the field he could see what looked like a smudge on the far horizon.

He walked until dark, then made himself a nest in the dead stalks, and went to sleep.

*H*e lay on his back, looking up at pink dawn clouds. Around him, dry stalks rustled in a faint stir of air. He felt crumbly earth under his fingers. He sat up, reached out and broke off a stalk. It crumbled into fragile chips. He wondered what it was. It wasn't any crop he'd ever seen before.

He stood, looked around. The field went on and on, dead flat. A locust came whirring toward him, plumped to earth at his feet. He picked it up. Long elbowed legs groped at his fingers aimlessly. He tossed the insect in the air. It fluttered away. To the east the smudge was clearer now; it seemed to be a grey wall, far away. A city? He picked up his bag and started on.

He was getting hungry. He hadn't eaten since the previous morning. He was thirsty too. The city couldn't be more than three hours' walk. He tramped along, the dry plants crackling under his feet, little puffs of dust rising from the dry ground. He thought about the rails, running across the empty fields, ending . . .

He had heard the locomotive groaning up ahead as the train slowed. And there had been feet in the corridor. Where had they gone?

He thought of the train, Casperton, Aunt Haicey, Mr. Phillips. They seemed very far away, something remembered from long ago. Up above the sun was hot. That was real. The rest seemed unimportant. Ahead there was a city. He would walk until he came to it. He tried to think of other things: television, crowds of people, money: the tattered paper and the worn silver —

Only the sun and the dusty plain and the dead plants were real now. He could see them, feel them. And the suitcase. It was heavy; he shifted hands, kept going.

There was something white on the ground ahead, a small shiny surface protruding from the earth. Brett dropped the suitcase, went down on one knee, dug into the dry soil, pulled out a china teacup, the handle missing. Caked dirt crumbled away under his thumb, leaving the surface clean. He looked at the bottom of the cup. It was unmarked. Why just one teacup, he wondered, here in the middle of nowhere? He dropped it, took up his suitcase, and went on.

*A*fter that he watched the ground more closely. He found a shoe; it was badly weathered, but the sole was good. It was a high-topped work shoe, size 10–1/2-C. Who had dropped it here? He thought of other lone shoes he had seen, lying at the roadside or in alleys. How did they get there. . . ?

Half an hour later he detoured around the rusted front fender of an old-fashioned car. He looked around for the rest of the car but saw nothing. The wall was closer now; perhaps five miles more.

A scrap of white paper fluttered across the field in a stir of air. He saw another, more, blowing along in the fitful gusts. He ran a few steps, caught one, smoothed it out.

BUY NOW — PAY LATER!

He picked up another.

PREPARE TO MEET GOD

A third said:

Win with Willkie

The wall loomed above him, smooth and grey. Dust was caked on his skin and clothes, and as he walked he brushed at himself absently. The suitcase dragged at his arm, thumped against his shin. He was very hungry and thirsty. He sniffed the air, instinctively searching for the odors of food. He had been following the wall for a long time, searching for an opening. It curved away from him, rising vertically from the level earth. Its surface was porous, unadorned, too smooth to climb. It was, Brett estimated, twenty feet high. If there were anything to make a ladder from —

Ahead he saw a wide gate, flanked by grey columns. He came up to it, put the suitcase down, and wiped at his forehead with his handkerchief. Through the opening in the wall a paved street was visible, and the façades of buildings. Those on the street before him were low, not more than one or two stories, but behind them taller towers reared up. There were no people in sight; no sounds stirred the hot noon-time air. Brett picked up his bag and passed through the gate.

For the next hour he walked empty pavements, listening to the echoes of his footsteps against brownstone fronts, empty shop windows, curtained glass doors, and here and there a vacant lot, weed-grown and desolate. He paused at cross streets, looked down long vacant ways. Now and then a distant sound came to him: the lonely honk of a horn, a faintly tolling bell, a clatter of hooves.

He came to a narrow alley that cut like a dark canyon between blank walls. He stood at its mouth, listening to a distant murmur, like a crowd at a funeral. He turned down the narrow way.

It went straight for a few yards, then twisted. As he followed its turnings the crowd noise gradually grew louder. He could make out individual voices now, an occasional word above the hubbub. He started to hurry, eager to find someone to talk to.

Abruptly the voices — hundreds of voices, he thought — rose in a roar, a long-drawn Yaaayyyyy. . . ! Brett thought of a stadium crowd as the home team trotted onto the field. He could hear a band now, a shrilling of brass, the clatter and thump of percussion instruments. Now he could see the mouth of the alley ahead, a sunny street hung with bunting, the backs of people, and over their heads the rhythmic bobbing of a passing procession, tall shakos and guidons in almost-even rows. Two tall poles with a streamer between them swung into view. He caught a glimpse of tall red letters:

. . . For Our Side!

He moved closer, edged up behind the grey-backed crowd. A phalanx of yellow-tuniced men approached, walking stiffly, fez tassels swinging. A small boy darted out into the street, loped along at their side. The music screeched and wheezed. Brett tapped the man before him.

"What's it all about. . . ?"

He couldn't hear his own voice. The man ignored him. Brett moved along behind the crowd, looking for a vantage point or a thinning in the ranks. There seemed to be fewer people ahead. He came to the end of the crowd, moved on a few yards, stood at the curb. The yellow-jackets had passed now, and a group of round-thighed girls in satin blouses and black boots and white fur caps glided into view, silent, expressionless. As they reached a point fifty feet from Brett, they broke abruptly into a strutting prance, knees high, hips flirting, tossing shining batons high, catching them, twirling them, and up again . . .

Brett craned his neck, looking for TV cameras. The crowd lining the opposite side of the street stood in solid ranks, drably clad, eyes following the procession, mouths working. A fat man in a rumpled suit and a panama hat squeezed to the front, stood picking his teeth. Somehow, he seemed out of place among the others. Behind the spectators, the store fronts looked normal, dowdy brick and mismatched glass and oxidizing aluminum, dusty windows and cluttered displays of cardboard, a faded sign that read TODAY ONLY — PRICES SLASHED. To Brett's left the sidewalk stretched, empty. To his right the crowd was packed close, the shout rising and falling. Now a rank of blue-suited policemen followed the majorettes, swinging along silently. Behind them, over them, a piece of paper blew along the street. Brett turned to the man on his right.

"Pardon me. Can you tell me the name of this town?"

The man ignored him. Brett tapped the man's shoulder. "Hey! What town is this?"

The man took off his hat, whirled it overhead, then threw it up. It sailed away over the crowd, lost. Brett wondered briefly how people who threw their hats ever recovered them. But then, nobody he knew would throw his hat . . .

"You mind telling me the name of this place?" Brett said, as he took the man's arm, pulled. The man rotated toward Brett, leaning heavily against him. Brett stepped back. The man fell, lay stiffly, his arms moving, his eyes and mouth open.

"Ahhhhh," he said. "Whum-whum-whum. Awww, jawww . . ."

Brett stooped quickly. "I'm sorry," he cried. He looked around. "Help! This man . . ."

Nobody was watching. The next man, a few feet away, stood close against his neighbor, hatless, his jaw moving.

"This man's sick," said Brett, tugging at the man's arm. "He fell."

The man's eyes moved reluctantly to Brett. "None of my business," he muttered.

"Won't anybody give me a hand?"

"Probably a drunk."

Behind Brett a voice called in a penetrating whisper: "Quick! You! Get into the alley. . . !"

He turned. A gaunt man of about thirty with sparse reddish hair, perspiration glistening on his upper lip, stood at the mouth of a narrow way like the one Brett had come through. He wore a grimy pale yellow shirt with a wide-flaring collar, limp and sweat-stained, dark green knee-breeches, soft leather boots, scuffed and dirty, with limp tops that drooped over his ankles. He gestured, drew back into the alley. "In here."

Brett went toward him. "This man . . ."

"Come on, you fool!" The man took Brett's arm, pulled him deeper into the dark passage. Brett resisted. "Wait a minute. That fellow . . ." He tried to point.

"Don't you know yet?" The red-head spoke with a strange accent. "Golems . . . You got to get out of sight before the —"

*T*he man froze, flattened himself against the wall. Automatically Brett moved to a place beside him. The man's head was twisted toward the alley mouth. The tendons in his weathered neck stood out. He had a three-day stubble of beard. Brett could smell him, standing this close. He edged away. "What —"

"Don't make a sound! Don't move, you idiot!" His voice was a thin hiss.

Brett followed the other's eyes toward the sunny street. The fallen man lay on the pavement, moving feebly, eyes open. Something moved up to him, a translucent brownish shape, like muddy water. It hovered for a moment, then dropped on the man like a breaking wave, flowed around him. The body shifted, rotating stiffly, then tilted upright. The sun struck through the fluid shape that flowed down now, amber highlights twinkling, to form itself into the crested wave, flow away.

"What the hell. . . !"

"Come on!" The red-head turned, trotted silently toward the shadowy bend under the high grey walls. He looked back, beckoned impatiently, passed out of sight around the turn —

Brett came up behind him, saw a wide avenue, tall trees with chartreuse springtime leaves, a wrought-iron fence, and beyond it, rolling green lawns. There were no people in sight.

"Wait a minute! What is this place?!"

His companion turned red-rimmed eyes on Brett. "How long have you been here?" he asked. "How did you get in?"

"I came through a gate. Just about an hour ago."

"I knew you were a man as soon as I saw you talking to the golem," said the red-head. "I've been here two months; maybe more. We've got to get out of sight. You want food? There's a place . . ." He jerked his thumb. "Come on. Time to talk later."

*B*rett followed him. They turned down a side street, pushed through the door of a dingy café. It banged behind them. There were tables, stools at a bar, a dusty juke box. They took seats at a table. The red-head groped under the table, pulled off a shoe, hammered it against the wall. He cocked his head, listening. The silence was absolute. He hammered again. There was a clash of crockery from beyond the kitchen door. "Now don't say anything," the red-head said. He eyed the door behind the counter expectantly. It flew open. A girl with red cheeks and untidy hair, dressed in a green waitress' uniform appeared, swept up to the table, pad and pencil in hand.

"Coffee and a ham sandwich," said the red-head. Brett said nothing. The girl glanced at him briefly, jotted hastily, whisked away.

"I saw them here the first day," the red-head said. "It was a piece of luck. I saw how the Gels started it up. They were big ones — not like the tidiers-up. As soon as they were finished, I came in and tried the same thing. It worked. I used the golem's lines —"

"I don't know what you're talking about," Brett said. "I'm going to ask that girl —"

"Don't say anything to her; it might spoil everything. The whole sequence might collapse; or it might call the Gels. I'm not sure. You can have the food when it comes back with it."

"Why do you say 'when "it" comes back'?"

"Ah." He looked at Brett strangely. "I'll show you."

Brett could smell food now. His mouth watered. He hadn't eaten for twenty-four hours.

"Care, that's the thing," the red-head said. "Move quiet, and stay out of sight, and you can live like a County Duke. Food's the hardest, but here —"

The red-cheeked girl reappeared, a tray balanced on one arm, a heavy cup and saucer in the other hand. She clattered them down on the table.

"Took you long enough," the red-head said. The girl sniffed, opened her mouth to speak — and the red-head darted out a stiff finger, jabbed her under the ribs. She stood, mouth open, frozen.

Brett half rose. "He's crazy, miss," he said. "Please accept —"

"Don't waste your breath." Brett's host was looking at him triumphantly. "Why do I call it 'it'?" He stood up, reached out and undid the top buttons of the green uniform. The waitress stood, leaning slightly forward, unmoving. The blouse fell open, exposing round white breasts — unadorned, blind.

"A doll," said the red-head. "A puppet; a golem."

*B*rett stared at her, the damp curls at her temple, the tip of her tongue behind her teeth, the tiny red veins in her round cheeks, and the white skin curving . . .

"That's a quick way to tell 'em," said the red-head. "The teat is smooth." He rebuttoned the uniform, then jabbed again at the girl's ribs. She straightened, patted her hair.

"No doubt a gentleman like you is used to better," she said carelessly. She went away.

"I'm Awalawon Dhuva," the red-head said.

"My name's Brett Hale." Brett took a bite of the sandwich.

"Those clothes," Dhuva said. "And you have a strange way of talking. What county are you from?"

"Jefferson."

"Never heard of it. I'm from Wavly. What brought you here?"

"I was on a train. The tracks came to an end out in the middle of nowhere. I walked . . . and here I am. What is this place?"

"Don't know." Dhuva shook his head. "I knew they were lying about the Fire River, though. Never did believe all that stuff. Religious hokum, to keep the masses quiet. Don't know what to believe now. Take the roof. They say a hundred kharfads up; but how do we know? Maybe it's a thousand — or only ten. By Grat, I'd like to go up in a balloon, see for myself."

"What are you talking about?" Brett said. "Go where in a balloon? See what?"

"Oh, I've seen one at the Tourney. Big hot-air bag, with a basket under it. Tied down with a rope. But if you cut the rope. . . ! But you can bet the priests will never let that happen, no, sir." Dhuva looked at Brett speculatively. "What about your county: Fession, or whatever you called it. How high do they tell you it is there?"

"You mean the sky? Well, the air ends after a few miles and space just goes on — millions of miles —"

Dhuva slapped the table and laughed. "The people in Fesseron must be some yokels! Just goes on up; now who'd swallow that tale?" He chuckled.

"Only a child thinks the sky is some kind of tent," said Brett. "Haven't you ever heard of the Solar System, the other planets?"

"What are those?"

"Other worlds. They all circle around the sun, like the Earth."

"Other worlds, eh? Sailing around up under the roof? Funny; I never saw them." Dhuva snickered. "Wake up, Brett. Forget all those stories. Just believe what you see."

"What about that brown thing?"

"The Gels? They run this place. Look out for them, Brett. Stay alert. Don't let them see you."

"What do they do?"

"I don't know — and I don't want to find out. This is a great place — I like it here. I have all I want to eat, plenty of nice rooms for sleeping. There's the parades and the scenes. It's a good life — as long as you keep out of sight."

"How do you get out of here?" Brett asked, finishing his coffee.

"Don't know how to get out; over the wall, I suppose. I don't plan to leave though. I left home in a hurry. The Duke — never mind. I'm not going back."

"Are all the people here . . . golems?" Brett said. "Aren't there anymore real people?"

"You're the first I've seen. I spotted you as soon as I saw you. A live man moves different than a golem. You see golems doing things like knitting their brows, starting back in alarm, looking askance, and standing arms akimbo. And they have things like pursed lips and knowing glances and mirthless laughter. You know: all the things you read about, that real people never do. But now that you're here, I've got somebody to talk to. I did get lonesome, I admit. I'll show you where I stay and we'll fix you up with a bed."

"I won't be around that long."

"What can you get outside that you can't get here? There's everything you need here in the city. We can have a great time."

"You sound like my Aunt Haicey," Brett said. "She said I had everything I needed back in Casperton. How does she know what I need? How do you know? How do I know myself? I can tell you I need more than food and a place to sleep —"

"What more?"

"Everything. Things to think about and something worth doing. Why, even in the movies —"

"What's a movie?"

"You know, a play, on film. A moving picture."

"A picture that moves?"

"That's right."

"This is something the priests told you about?" Dhuva seemed to be holding in his mirth.

"Everybody's seen movies."

Dhuva burst out laughing. "Those priests," he said. "They're the same everywhere, I see. The stories they tell, and people believe them. What else?"

"Priests have nothing to do with it."

Dhuva composed his features. "What do they tell you about Grat, and the Wheel?"

"Grat? What's that?"

"The Over-Being. The Four-eyed One." Dhuva made a sign, caught himself. "Just habit," he said. "I don't believe that rubbish. Never did."

"I suppose you're talking about God," Brett said.

"I don't know about God. Tell me about it."

"He's the creator of the world. He's . . . well, super-human. He knows everything that happens, and when you die, if you've led a good life, you meet God in Heaven."

"Where's that?"

"It's . . ." Brett waved a hand vaguely, "up above."

"But you said there was just emptiness up above," Dhuva recalled. "And some other worlds whirling around, like islands adrift in the sea."

"Well —"

"Never mind," Dhuva held up his hands. "Our priests are liars too. All that balderdash about the

Wheel and the River of Fire. It's just as bad as your Hivvel or whatever you called it. And our Grat and your Mud, or Gog: they're the same —" Dhuva's head went up. "What's that?"

"I didn't hear anything."

*D*huva got to his feet, turned to the door. Brett rose. A towering brown shape, glassy and transparent, hung in the door, its surface rippling. Dhuva whirled, leaped past Brett, dived for the rear door. Brett stood frozen. The shape flowed — swift as quicksilver — caught Dhuva in mid-stride, engulfed him. For an instant Brett saw the thin figure, legs kicking, upended within the muddy form of the Gel. Then the turbid wave swept across to the door, sloshed it aside, disappeared. Dhuva was gone.

Brett stood rooted, staring at the doorway. A bar of sunlight fell across the dusty floor. A brown mouse ran along the baseboard. It was very quiet. Brett went to the door through which the Gel had disappeared, hesitated a moment, then thrust it open.

He was looking down into a great dark pit, acres in extent, its sides riddled with holes, the amputated ends of water and sewage lines and power cables dangling. Far below light glistened from the surface of a black pool. A few feet away the waitress stood unmoving in the dark on a narrow strip of linoleum. At her feet the chasm yawned. The edge of the floor was ragged, as though it had been gnawed away by rats. There was no sign of Dhuva.

Brett stepped back into the dining room, let the door swing shut. He took a deep breath, picked up a paper napkin from a table and wiped his forehead, dropped the napkin on the floor and went out into the street, his suitcase forgotten now. At the corner he turned, walked along past silent shop windows crowded with home permanents, sun glasses, fingernail polish, sun-tan lotion, paper cartons, streamers, plastic toys, vari-colored garments of synthetic fiber, home remedies, beauty aids, popular music, greeting cards . . .

At the next corner he stopped, looking down the silent streets. Nothing moved. Brett went to a window in a grey concrete wall, pulled himself up to peer through the dusty pane, saw a room filled with tailor's forms, garment racks, a bicycle, bundled back issues of magazines without covers.

He went along to a door. It was solid, painted shut. The next door looked easier. He wrenched at the tar-nished brass knob, then stepped back and kicked the door. With a hollow sound the door fell inward, taking with it the jamb. Brett stood staring at the gaping opening. A fragment of masonry dropped with a dry clink. Brett stepped through the breach in the grey façade. The black pool at the bottom of the pit winked a flicker of light back at him in the deep gloom.

*A*round him, the high walls of the block of buildings loomed in silhouette; the squares of the windows were ranks of luminous blue against the dark. Dust motes danced in shafts of sunlight. Far above, the roof was dimly visible, a spidery tangle of trusswork. And below was the abyss.

At Brett's feet the stump of a heavy brass rail pro-jected an inch from the floor. It was long enough, Brett thought, to give firm anchor to a rope. Somewhere below, Dhuva — a stranger who had befriended him — lay in the grip of the Gels. He would do what he could

— but he needed equipment — and help. First he would find a store with rope, guns, knives. He would —

The broken edge of masonry where the door had been caught his eye. The shell of the wall, exposed where the door frame had torn away, was wafer-thin. Brett reached up, broke off a piece. The outer face — the side that showed on the street — was smooth, solid-looking. The back was porous, nibbled. Brett stepped outside, examined the wall. He kicked at the grey surface. A great piece of wall, six feet high, broke into fragments, fell on the sidewalk with a crash, driving out a puff of dust. Another section fell. One piece of it skidded away, clattered down into the depths. Brett heard a distant splash. He looked at the great jagged opening in the wall — like a jigsaw picture with a piece missing. He turned and started off at a trot, his mouth dry, his pulse thumping painfully in his chest.

Two blocks from the hollow building, Brett slowed to a walk, his footsteps echoing in the empty street. He looked into each store window as he passed. There were artificial legs, bottles of colored water, immense dolls, wigs, glass eyes — but no rope. Brett tried to think. What kind of store would handle rope? A marine supply company, maybe. But where would he find one?

Perhaps it would be easiest to look in a telephone book. Ahead he saw a sign lettered HOTEL. Brett went up to the revolving door, pushed inside. He was in a dim, marble-paneled lobby, with double doors leading into a beige-carpeted bar on his right, the brass-painted cage of an elevator directly before him, flanked by tall urns of sand and an ascending staircase. On the left was a dark mahogany-finished reception desk. Behind the desk a man stood silently, waiting. Brett felt a wild surge of relief.

"Those things, those Gels!" he called, starting across the room. "My friend —"

He broke off. The clerk stood, staring over Brett's shoulder, holding a pen poised over a book. Brett reached out, took the pen. The man's finger curled stiffly around nothing. A golem.

*B*rett turned away, went into the bar. Vacant stools were ranged before a dark mirror. At the tables empty glasses stood before empty chairs. Brett started as he heard the revolving door thump-thump. Suddenly soft light bathed the lobby behind him. Somewhere a piano tinkled *More Than You Know.* With a distant clatter of closing doors the elevator came to life.

Brett hugged a shadowed corner, saw a fat man in a limp seersucker suit cross to the reception desk. He had a red face, a bald scalp blotched with large brown freckles. The clerk inclined his head blandly.

"Ah, yes, sir, a nice double with bath . . ." Brett heard the unctuous voice of the clerk as he offered the pen. The fat man took it, scrawled something in the register. ". . . at fourteen dollars," the clerk murmured. He smiled, dinged the bell. A boy in tight green tunic and trousers and a pillbox cap with a chin strap pushed through a door beside the desk, took the key, led the way to the elevator. The fat man entered. Through the openwork of the shaft Brett watched as the elevator car rose, greasy cables trembling and swaying. He started back across the lobby — and stopped dead.

A wet brown shape had appeared in the entrance. It flowed across the rug to the bellhop. Face blank, the golem turned back to its door. Above, Brett heard the elevator stop. Doors clashed. The clerk stood poised behind the desk. The Gel hovered, then flowed away. The piano was silent now. The lights burned, a soft glow, then winked out. Brett thought about the fat man. He had seen him before . . .

He went up the stairs. In the second floor corridor Brett felt his way along in near-darkness, guided by the dim light coming through transoms. He tried a door. It opened. He stepped into a large bedroom with a double bed, an easy chair, a chest of drawers. He crossed the room, looked out across an alley. Twenty feet away white curtains hung at windows in a brick wall. There was nothing behind the windows.

There were sounds in the corridor. Brett dropped to the floor behind the bed.

"All right, you two," a drunken voice bellowed. "And may all your troubles be little ones." There was laughter, squeals, a dry clash of beads flung against the door. A key grated. The door swung wide. Lights blazed in the hall, silhouetting the figures of a man in black jacket and trousers, a woman in a white bridal dress and veil, flowers in her hand.

"Take care, Mel!"

". . . do anything I wouldn't do!"

". . . kiss the bride, now!"

The couple backed into the room, pushed the door shut, stood against it. Brett crouched behind the bed, not breathing, waiting. The couple stood at the door, in the dark, heads down . . .

*B*rett stood, rounded the foot of the bed, approached the two unmoving figures. The girl looked young, sleek, perfect-featured, with soft dark hair. Her eyes were half-open; Brett caught a glint of light reflected from the eyeball. The man was bronzed, broad-shouldered, his hair wavy and blond. His lips were parted, showing even white teeth. The two stood, not breathing, sightless eyes fixed on nothing.

Brett took the bouquet from the woman's hand. The flowers seemed real — except that they had no perfume. He dropped them on the floor, pulled at the male golem to clear the door. The figure pivoted, toppled, hit with a heavy thump. Brett raised the woman in his arms and propped her against the bed. Back at the door he listened. All was quiet now. He started to open the door, then hesitated. He went back to the bed, undid the tiny pearl buttons down the front of the bridal gown, pulled it open. The breasts were rounded, smooth, an unbroken creamy white . . .

In the hall, he started toward the stair. A tall Gel rippled into view ahead, its shape flowing and wavering, now billowing out, then rising up. The shifting form undulated toward Brett. He made a move to run, then remembered Dhuva, stood motionless. The Gel wobbled past him, slumped suddenly, flowed under a door. Brett let out a breath. Never mind the fat man. There were too many Gels here. He started back along the corridor.

Soft music came from double doors which stood open on a landing. Brett went to them, risked a look inside. Graceful couples moved sedately on a polished floor, diners sat at tables, black-clad waiters moving among them. At the far side of the room, near a dusty rubber plant, sat the fat man, studying a menu. As Brett watched he shook out a napkin, ran it around inside his collar, then mopped his face.

Never disturb a scene, Dhuva had said. But perhaps he could blend with it. Brett brushed at his suit, straightened his tie, stepped into the room. A waiter approached, eyed him dubiously. Brett got out his wallet, took out a five-dollar bill.

"A quiet table in the corner," he said. He glanced back. There were no Gels in sight. He followed the waiter to a table near the fat man.

*S*eated, he looked around. He wanted to talk to the fat man, but he couldn't afford to attract attention. He would watch, and wait his chance.

At the nearby tables men with well-pressed suits, clean collars, and carefully shaved faces murmured to sleekly gowned women who fingered wine glasses, smiled archly. He caught fragments of conversation:

"My dear, have you heard . . ."

". . . in the low eighties . . ."

". . . quite impossible. One must . . ."

". . . for this time of year."

The waiter returned with a shallow bowl of milky soup. Brett looked at the array of spoons, forks, knives, glanced sideways at the diners at the next table. It was important to follow the correct ritual. He put his napkin in his lap, careful to shake out all the folds. He looked at the spoons again, picked a large one, glanced at the waiter. So far so good . . .

"Wine, sir?"

Brett indicated the neighboring couple. "The same as they're having." The waiter turned away, returned holding a wine bottle, label toward Brett. He looked at it, nodded. The waiter busied himself with the cork, removing it with many flourishes, setting a glass before Brett, pouring half an inch of wine. He waited expectantly.

Brett picked up the glass, tasted it. It tasted like wine. He nodded. The waiter poured. Brett wondered what would have happened if he had made a face and spurned it. But it would be too risky to try. No one ever did it.

Couples danced, resumed their seats; others rose and took the floor. A string ensemble in a distant corner played restrained tunes that seemed to speak of the gentle faded melancholy of decorous tea dances on long-forgotten afternoons. Brett glanced toward the fat man. He was eating soup noisily, his napkin tied under his chin.

The waiter was back with a plate. "Lovely day, sir," he said.

"Great," Brett agreed.

The waiter placed a covered platter on the table, removed the cover, stood with carving knife and fork poised.

"A bit of the crispy, sir?"

Brett nodded. He eyed the waiter surreptitiously. He looked real. Some golems seemed realer than others; or perhaps it merely depended on the parts they were playing. The man who had fallen at the parade had been only a sort of extra, a crowd member. The waiter, on the other hand, was able to converse. Perhaps it would be possible to learn something from him . . .

"What's . . . uh . . . how do you spell the name of this town?" Brett asked.

"I was never much of a one for spelling, sir," the waiter said.

"Try it."

"Gravy, sir?"

"Sure. Try to spell the name."

"Perhaps I'd better call the headwaiter, sir," the golem said stiffly.

From the corner of an eye Brett caught a flicker of motion. He whirled, saw nothing. Had it been a Gel?

"Never mind," he said. The waiter served potatoes, peas, refilled the wine glass, moved off silently. The question had been a little too unorthodox, Brett decided. Perhaps if he led up to the subject more obliquely . . .

*W*hen the waiter returned Brett said, "Nice day."

"Very nice, sir."

"Better than yesterday."

"Yes indeed, sir."

"I wonder what tomorrow'll be like."

"Perhaps we'll have a bit of rain, sir."

Brett nodded toward the dance floor. "Nice orchestra."

"They're very popular, sir."

"From here in town?"

"I wouldn't know as to that, sir."

"Lived here long yourself?"

"Oh, yes, sir." The waiter's expression showed disapproval. "Would there be anything else, sir?"

"I'm a newcomer here," Brett said. "I wonder if you could tell me —"

"Excuse me, sir." The waiter was gone. Brett poked at the mashed potatoes. Quizzing golems was hopeless. He would have to find out for himself. He turned to look at the fat man. As Brett watched he took a large handkerchief from a pocket, blew his nose loudly. No one turned to look. The orchestra played softly. The couples danced. Now was as good a time as any . . .

Brett rose, crossed to the other's table. The man looked up.

"Mind if I sit down?" Brett said. "I'd like to talk to you."

The fat man blinked, motioned to a chair. Brett sat down, leaned across the table. "Maybe I'm wrong," he said quietly, "but I think you're real."

The fat man blinked again. "What's that?" he snapped. He had a high petulant voice.

"You're not like the rest of them. I think I can talk to you. I think you're another outsider."

The fat man looked down at his rumpled suit. "I . . . ah . . . was caught a little short today. Didn't have time to change. I'm a busy man. And what business is it of yours?" He clamped his jaw shut, eyed Brett warily.

"I'm a stranger here," Brett said. "I want to find out what's going on in this place —"

"Buy an amusement guide. Lists all the shows —"

"I don't mean that. I mean these dummies all over the place, and the Gels —"

"What dummies? Jells? Jello? You don't like Jello?"

"I love Jello. I don't —"

"Just ask the waiter. He'll bring you your Jello. Any flavor you like. Now if you'll excuse me . . ."

"I'm talking about the brown things; they look like muddy water. They come around if you interfere with a scene."

The fat man looked nervous. "Please. Go away."

"If I make a disturbance, the Gels will come. Is that what you're afraid of?"

"Now, now. Be calm. No need for you to get excited."

"I won't make a scene," Brett said. "Just talk to me. How long have you been here?"

"I dislike scenes. I dislike them intensely."

"When did you come here?"

"Just ten minutes ago. I just sat down. I haven't had my dinner yet. Please, young man. Go back to your table." The fat man watched Brett warily. Sweat glistened on his bald head.

"I mean this town. How long have you been here? Where did you come from?"

"Why, I was born here. Where did I come from? What sort of question is that? Just consider that the stork brought me."

"You were born here?"

"Certainly."

"What's the name of the town?"

"*A*re you trying to make a fool of me?" The fat man was getting angry. His voice was rising.

"Shhh," Brett cautioned. "You'll attract the Gels."

"Blast the Jilts, whatever that is!" the fat man snapped. "Now, get along with you. I'll call the manager."

"Don't you know?" Brett said, staring at the fat man. "They're all dummies; golems, they're called. They're not real."

"Who're not real?"

"All these imitation people at the tables and on the dance floor. Surely you realize —"

"I realize you're in need of medical attention." The fat man pushed back his chair and got to his feet. "You keep the table," he said. "I'll dine elsewhere."

"Wait!" Brett got up, seized the fat man's arm.

"Take your hands off me —" The fat man went toward the door. Brett followed. At the cashier's desk Brett turned suddenly, saw a fluid brown shape flicker —

"Look!" He pulled at the fat man's arm —

"Look at what?" The Gel was gone.

"It was there: a Gel."

The fat man flung down a bill, hurried away. Brett fumbled out a ten, waited for change. "Wait!" he called. He heard the fat man's feet receding down the stairs.

"Hurry," he said to the cashier. The woman sat glassy-eyed, staring at nothing. The music died. The lights flickered, went off. In the gloom Brett saw a fluid shape rise up —

He ran, pounding down the stairs. The fat man was just rounding the corner. Brett opened his mouth to call — and went rigid, as a translucent shape of mud shot from the door, rose up to tower before him. Brett stood, mouth half open, eyes staring, leaning forward with hands outflung. The Gel loomed, its surface flickering — waiting. Brett caught an acrid odor of geraniums.

A minute passed. Brett's cheek itched. He fought a desire to blink, to swallow — to turn and run. The high sun beat down on the silent street, the still window displays.

Then the Gel broke form, slumped, flashed away. Brett tottered back against the wall, let his breath out in a harsh sigh.

Across the street he saw a window with a display of camping equipment, portable stoves, boots, rifles. He crossed the street, tried the door. It was locked. He looked up and down the street. There was no one in sight. He kicked in the glass beside the latch, reached through and turned the knob. Inside he looked over the shelves, selected a heavy coil of nylon rope, a sheath knife, a canteen. He examined a Winchester repeating rifle with a telescopic sight, then put it back and strapped on a .22 revolver. He emptied two boxes of long rifle cartridges into his pocket, then loaded the pistol. He coiled the rope over his shoulder and went back out into the empty street.

*T*he fat man was standing in front of a shop in the next block, picking at a blemish on his chin and eyeing the window display. He looked up with a frown, started away as Brett came up.

"Wait a minute," Brett called. "Didn't you see the Gel? the one that cornered me back there?"

The fat man looked back suspiciously, kept going.

"Wait!" Brett caught his arm. "I know you're real. I've seen you belch and sweat and scratch. You're the only one I can call on — and I need help. My friend is trapped —"

The fat man pulled away, his face flushed an even deeper red. "I'm warning you, you maniac: get away from me. . . !"

Brett stepped close, rammed the fat man hard in the ribs. He sank to his knees, gasping. The panama hat rolled away. Brett grabbed his arm, steadied him.

"Sorry," he said. "I had to be sure. You're real, all right. We've got to rescue my friend, Dhuva —"

The fat man leaned against the glass, rolling terrified eyes, rubbing his stomach. "I'll call the police!" he gasped.

"What police?" Brett waved an arm. "Look. Not a car in sight. Did you ever see the street that empty before?"

"Wednesday afternoon," the fat man gasped.

"Come with me. I want to show you. It's all hollow. There's nothing behind these walls —"

"Why doesn't somebody come along?" the fat man moaned.

"The masonry is only a quarter-inch thick," Brett said. "Come on; I'll show you."

"I don't like it," said the fat man. His face was pale and moist. "You're mad. What's wrong? It's so quiet . . ."

"We've got to try to save him. The Gel took him down into this pit —"

"Let me go," the man whined. "I'm afraid. Can't you just let me lead my life in peace?"

"Don't you understand? The Gel took a man. They may be after you next."

"There's no one after me! I'm a business man . . . a respectable citizen. I mind my own business, give to charity, go to church. All I want is to be left alone!"

*B*rett dropped his hands from the fat man's arms, stood looking at him: the blotched face, pale now, the damp forehead, the quivering jowls. The fat man stooped for his hat, slapped it against his leg, clamped it on his head.

"I think I understand now," said Brett. "This is your place, this imitation city. Everything's faked to fit your needs — like in the hotel. Wherever you go, the scene unrolls in front of you. You never see the Gels, never discover the secret of the golems — because you conform. You never do the unexpected."

"That's right. I'm law-abiding. I'm respectable. I don't pry. I don't nose into other people's business. Why should I? Just let me alone . . ."

"Sure," Brett said. "Even if I dragged you down there and showed you, you wouldn't believe it. But you're not in the scene now. I've taken you out of it —"

Suddenly the fat man turned and ran a few yards, then looked back to see whether Brett was pursuing him. He shook a round fist.

"I've seen your kind before," he shouted. "Trouble-makers."

Brett took a step toward him. The fat man yelped and ran another fifty feet, his coat tails bobbing. He looked back, stopped, a fat figure alone in the empty sunny street.

"You haven't seen the last of me!" he shouted. "We know how to deal with your kind." He tugged at his vest, went off along the sidewalk. Brett watched him go, then started back toward the hollow building.

*T*he jagged fragments of masonry Brett had knocked from the wall lay as he had left them. He stepped through the opening, peered down into the murky pit, trying to judge its depth. A hundred feet at least. Perhaps a hundred and fifty.

He unslung the rope from his shoulder, tied one end to the brass stump, threw the coil down the precipitous side. It fell away into darkness, hung swaying. It was impossible to tell whether the end reached any solid footing below. He couldn't waste anymore time looking for help. He would have to try it alone.

There was a scrape of shoe leather on the pavement outside. He turned, stepped out into the white sunlight. The fat man rounded the corner, recoiled as he saw Brett. He flung out a pudgy forefinger, his protruding eyes wide in his blotchy red face.

"There he is! I told you he came this way!" Two uniformed policemen came into view. One eyed the gun at Brett's side, put a hand on his own.

"Better take that off, sir."

"Look!" Brett said to the fat man. He stooped, picked up a crust of masonry. "Look at this — just a shell —"

"He's blasted a hole right in that building, officer!" the fat man shrilled. "He's dangerous."

The cop ignored the gaping hole in the wall. "You'll have to come along with me, sir. This gentleman registered a complaint . . ."

Brett stood staring into the cop's eyes. They were pale blue eyes, looking steadily back at him from a bland face. Could the cop be real? Or would he be able to push him over, as he had other golems?

"The fellow's not right in the head," the fat man was saying to the cop. "You should have heard his crazy talk. A troublemaker. His kind have got to be locked up!"

The cop nodded. "Can't have anyone causing trouble."

"Only a young fellow," said the fat man. He mopped at his forehead with a large handkerchief. "Tragic. But I'm sure that you men know how to handle him."

"Better give me the gun, sir." The cop held out a hand. Brett moved suddenly, rammed stiff fingers into the cop's ribs. He stiffened, toppled, lay rigid, staring up at nothing.

"You . . . you killed him," the fat man gasped, backing. The second cop tugged at his gun. Brett leaped at him, sent him down with a blow to the ribs. He turned to face the fat man.

"I didn't kill them! I just turned them off. They're not real, they're just golems."

"A killer! And right in the city, in broad daylight."

"You've got to help me!" Brett cried. "This whole scene: don't you see? It has the air of something improvised in a hurry, to deal with the unexpected factor; that's me. The Gels know something's wrong, but they can't quite figure out what. When you called the cops the Gels obliged —"

Startlingly the fat man burst into tears. He fell to his knees.

"Don't kill me . . . oh, don't kill me . . ."

"Nobody's going to kill you, you fool!" Brett snapped. "Look! I want to show you!" He seized the fat man's lapel, dragged him to his feet and across the sidewalk, through the opening. The fat man stopped dead, stumbled back —

"What's this? What kind of place is this?" He scrambled for the opening.

"It's what I've been trying to tell you. This city you live in — it's a hollow shell. There's nothing inside. None of it's real. Only you . . . and me. There was another man: Dhuva. I was in a café with him. A Gel came. He tried to run. It caught him. Now he's . . . down there."

"I'm not alone," the fat man babbled. "I have my friends, my clubs, my business associates. I'm insured. Lately I've been thinking a lot about Jesus —"

He broke off, whirled, and jumped for the doorway. Brett leaped after him, caught his coat. It ripped. The fat man stumbled over one of the cop-golems, went to hands and knees. Brett stood over him.

"Get up, damn it!" he snapped. "I need help and you're going to help me!" He hauled the fat man to his feet. "All you have to do is stand by the rope. Dhuva may be unconscious when I find him. You'll have to help me haul him up. If anybody comes along, any Gels, I mean — give me a signal. A whistle . . . like this —" Brett demonstrated. "And if I get in trouble, do what you can. Here . . ." Brett started to offer the fat man the gun, then handed him the hunting knife. "If anybody interferes, this may not do any good, but it's something. I'm going down now."

The fat man watched as Brett gripped the rope, let himself over the edge. Brett looked up at the glistening face, the damp strands of hair across the freckled scalp. Brett had no assurance that the man would stay at his post, but he had done what he could.

"Remember," said Brett. "It's a real man they've got, like you and me . . . not a golem. We owe it to him." The fat man's hands trembled. He watched Brett, licked his lips. Brett started down.

*T*he descent was easy. The rough face of the excavation gave footholds. The end of a decaying timber projected; below it was the stump of a crumbling concrete pipe two feet in diameter. Brett was ten feet below the rim of floor now. Above, the broad figure of the fat man was visible in silhouette against the jagged opening in the wall.

Now the cliff shelved back; the rope hung free. Brett eased past the cut end of a rusted water pipe, went down hand over hand. If there were nothing at the bottom to give him footing, it would be a long climb back . . .

Twenty feet below he could see the still black water, pockmarked with expanding rings where bits of debris dislodged by his passage peppered the surface.

There was a rhythmic vibration in the rope. Brett felt it through his hands, a fine sawing sensation . . .

He was falling, gripping the limp rope . . .

He slammed on his back in three feet of oily water. The coils of rope collapsed around him with a sustained splashing. He got to his feet, groped for the end of the rope. The glossy nylon strands had been cleanly cut.

*F*or half an hour Brett waded in waist-deep water along a wall of damp clay that rose sheer above him. Far above, bars of dim sunlight crossed the upper

reaches of the cavern. He had seen no sign of Dhuva
. . . or the Gels.

He encountered a sodden timber that projected
above the surface of the pool, clung to it to rest. Bits
of flotsam — a plastic pistol, bridge tallies, a golf bag
— floated in the black water. A tunnel extended
through the clay wall ahead; beyond, Brett could see a
second great cavern rising. He pictured the city, silent
and empty above, and the honey-combed earth beneath. He moved on.

An hour later Brett had traversed the second cavern.
Now he clung to an outthrust spur of granite directly
beneath the point at which Dhuva had disappeared.
Far above he could see the green-clad waitress standing
stiffly on her ledge. He was tired. Walking in water, his
feet floundering in soft mud, was exhausting. He was
no closer to escape, or to finding Dhuva, than he had
been when the fat man cut the rope. He had been a
fool to leave the man alone, with a knife . . . but he
had had no choice.

He would have to find another way out. Endlessly
wading at the bottom of the pit was useless. He would
have to climb. One spot was as good as another. He
stepped back and scanned the wall of clay looming
over him. Twenty feet up, water dripped from the
broken end of a four-inch water main. Brett uncoiled
the rope from his shoulder, tied a loop in the end,
whirled it and cast upward. It missed, fell back with a
splash. He gathered it in, tried again. On the third try
it caught. He tested it, then started up. His hands were
slippery with mud and water. He twined the rope
around his legs, inched higher. The slender cable was
smooth as glass. He slipped back two feet, then inched
upward, slipped again, painfully climbed, slipped,
climbed.

After the first ten feet he found toe-holds in the muddy wall. He worked his way up, his hands aching and raw. A projecting tangle of power cable gave a secure purchase for a foot. He rested. Nearby, an opening two feet in diameter gaped in the clay: a tunnel. It might be possible to swing sideways across the face of the clay and reach the opening. It was worth a try. His stiff, clay-slimed hands would pull him no higher.

He gripped the rope, kicked off sideways, hooked a foot in the tunnel mouth, half jumped, half fell into the mouth of the tunnel. He clung to the rope, shook it loose from the pipe above, coiled it and looped it over his shoulder. On hands and knees he started into the narrow passage.

*T*he tunnel curved left, then right, dipped, then angled up. Brett crawled steadily, the smooth stiff clay yielding and cold against his hands and sodden knees. Another smaller tunnel joined from the left. Another angled in from above. The tunnel widened to three feet, then four. Brett got to his feet, walked in a crouch. Here and there, barely visible in the near-darkness, objects lay imbedded in the mud: a silver-plated spoon, its handle bent; the rusted engine of an electric train; a portable radio, green with corrosion from burst batteries.

At a distance, Brett estimated, of a hundred yards from the pit, the tunnel opened into a vast cave, green-lit from tiny discs of frosted glass set in the ceiling far above. A row of discolored concrete piles, the foundations of the building above, protruded against the near wall, their surfaces nibbled and pitted. Between Brett and the concrete columns the floor was littered with pale sticks and stones, gleaming dully in the gloom.

Brett started across the floor. One of the sticks snapped underfoot. He kicked a melon-sized stone. It rolled lightly, came to rest with hollow eyes staring toward him. A human skull.

*T*he floor of the cave covered an area the size of a city block. It was blanketed with human bones, with here and there a small cat skeleton or the fanged snout-bones of a dog. There was a constant rustling of rats that played among the rib cages, sat atop crania, scuttled behind shin-bones. Brett picked his way, stepping over imitation pearl necklaces, zircon rings, plastic buttons, hearing aids, lipsticks, compacts, corset stays, prosthetic devices, rubber heels, wrist watches, lapel watches, pocket watches with corroded brass chains.

Ahead Brett saw a patch of color: a blur of pale yellow. He hurried, stumbling over bone heaps, crunching eyeglasses underfoot. He reached the still figure where it lay slackly, face down. Gingerly he squatted, turned it on its back. It was Dhuva.

Brett slapped the cold wrists, rubbed the clammy hands. Dhuva stirred, moaned weakly. Brett pulled him to a sitting position. "Wake up!" he whispered. "Wake up!"

Dhuva's eyelids fluttered. He blinked dully at Brett.

"The Gels may turn up any minute," Brett hissed. "We have to get away from here. Can you walk?"

"I saw it," said Dhuva faintly. "But it moved so fast . . ."

"You're safe here for the moment," Brett said. "There are none of them around. But they may be back. We've got to find a way out!"

Dhuva started up, staring around. "Where am I?" he said hoarsely. Brett seized his arm, steadied him on his feet.

"We're in a hollowed-out cave," he said. "The whole city is undermined with them. They're connected by tunnels. We have to find one leading back to the surface."

Dhuva gazed around at the acres of bones. "It left me here for dead."

"Or to die," said Brett.

"Look at them," Dhuva breathed. "Hundreds . . . thousands . . ."

"The whole population, it looks like. The Gels must have whisked them down here one by one."

"But why?"

"For interfering with the scenes. But that doesn't matter now. What matters is getting out. Come on. I see tunnels on the other side."

They crossed the broad floor, around them the white bones, the rustle of rats. They reached the far side of the cave, picked a six-foot tunnel which trended upward, a trickle of water seeping out of the dark mouth. They started up the slope.

"We have to have a weapon against the Gels," said Brett.

"Why? I don't want to fight them." Dhuva's voice was thin, frightened. "I want to get away from here . . . even back to Wavly. I'd rather face the Duke."

"This was a real town, once," said Brett. "The Gels have taken it over, hollowed out the buildings, mined the earth under it, killed off the people, and put imitation people in their place. And nobody ever knew. I met a man who's lived here all his life. He doesn't know. But we know . . . and we have to do something about it."

"It's not our business. I've had enough. I want to get away."

"The Gels must stay down below, somewhere in that maze of tunnels. For some reason they try to keep up appearances . . . but only for the people who belong here. They play out scenes for the fat man, wherever he goes. And he never goes anywhere he isn't expected to."

"We'll get over the wall somehow," said Dhuva. "We may starve, crossing the dry fields, but that's better than this."

They emerged from the tunnel into a coal bin, crossed to a sagging door, found themselves in a boiler room. Stairs led up to sunlight. In the street, in the shadow of tall buildings, a boxy sedan was parked at the curb. Brett went to it, tried the door. It opened. Keys dangled from the ignition switch. He slid into the dusty seat. Behind him there was a hoarse scream. Brett looked up. Through the streaked windshield he saw a mighty Gel rear up before Dhuva, who crouched back against the blackened brick front of the building.

"Don't move, Dhuva!" Brett shouted. Dhuva stood frozen, flattened against the wall. The Gel towered, its surface rippling.

Brett eased from the seat. He stood on the pavement, fifteen feet from the Gel. The rank Gel odor came in waves from the creature. Beyond it he could see Dhuva's white terrified face.

Silently Brett turned the latch of the old-fashioned auto hood, raised it. The copper fuel line curved down from the firewall to a glass sediment cup. The knurled

retaining screw turned easily; the cup dropped into
Brett's hand. Gasoline ran down in an amber stream.
Brett pulled off his damp coat, wadded it, jammed it
under the flow. Over his shoulder he saw Dhuva, still
rigid — and the Gel, hovering, uncertain.

The coat was saturated with gasoline now. Brett
fumbled a match box from his pocket. Wet. He threw
the sodden container aside. The battery caught his eye,
clamped in a rusted frame under the hood. He jerked
the pistol from its holster, used it to short the termi-
nals. Tiny blue sparks jumped. He jammed the coat
near, rasped the gun against the soft lead poles. With
a whoosh! the coat caught; yellow flames leaped, soot-
rimmed. Brett snatched at a sleeve, whirled the coat
high. The great Gel, attracted by the sudden motion,
rushed at him. He flung the blazing garment over the
monster, leaped aside.

The creature went mad. It slumped, lashed itself
against the pavement. The burning coat was thrown
clear. The Gel threw itself across the pavement, into
the gutter, sending a splatter of filthy water over Brett.
From the corner of his eye, Brett saw Dhuva seize the
burning coat, hurl it into the pooled gasoline in the
gutter. Fire leaped twenty feet high; in its center the
great Gel bucked and writhed. The ancient car shud-
dered as the frantic monster struck it. Black smoke
boiled up; an unbelievable stench came to Brett's nos-
trils. He backed, coughing. Flames roared around the
front of the car. Paint blistered and burned. A tire
burst. In a final frenzy, the Gel whipped clear, lay, a
great blackened shape of melting rubber, twitching,
then still.

"They've tunneled under everything," Brett said. "They've cut through power lines and water lines, concrete, steel, earth; they've left the shell, shored up with spidery-looking trusswork. Somehow they've kept water and power flowing to wherever they needed it —"

"I don't care about your theories," Dhuva said; "I only want to get away."

"It's bound to work, Dhuva. I need your help."

"No."

"Then I'll have to try alone." He turned away.

"Wait," Dhuva called. He came up to Brett. "I owe you a life; you saved mine. I can't let you down now. But if this doesn't work . . . or if you can't find what you want —"

"Then we'll go."

Together they turned down a side street, walking rapidly. At the next corner Brett pointed.

"There's one!" They crossed to the service station at a run. Brett tried the door. Locked. He kicked at it, splintered the wood around the lock. He glanced around inside. "No good," he called. "Try the next building. I'll check the one behind."

He crossed the wide drive, battered in a door, looked in at a floor covered with wood shavings. It ended ten feet from the door. Brett went to the edge, looked down. Diagonally, forty feet away, the underground fifty-thousand-gallon storage tank which supplied the gasoline pumps of the station perched, isolated, on a column of striated clay, ribbed with chitinous Gel buttresses. The truncated feed lines ended six feet from the tank. From Brett's position, it was impossible to say whether the ends were plugged.

Across the dark cavern a square of light appeared. Dhuva stood in a doorway looking toward Brett.

"Over here, Dhuva!" Brett uncoiled his rope, arranged a slip-noose. He measured the distance with his eye, tossed the loop. It slapped the top of the tank, caught on a massive fitting. He smashed the glass from a window, tied the end of the rope to the center post. Dhuva arrived, watched as Brett went to the edge, hooked his legs over the rope, and started across to the tank.

It was an easy crossing. Brett's feet clanged against the tank. He straddled the six-foot cylinder, worked his way to the end, then clambered down to the two two-inch feed lines. He tested their resilience, then lay flat, eased out on them. There were plugs of hard waxy material in the cut ends of the pipes. Brett poked at them with the pistol. Chunks loosened and fell. He worked for fifteen minutes before the first trickle came. Two minutes later, two thick streams of gasoline were pouring down into the darkness.

*B*rett and Dhuva piled sticks, scraps of paper, shavings, and lumps of coal around a core of gasoline-soaked rags. Directly above the heaped tinder a taut rope stretched from the window post to a child's wagon, the steel bed of which contained a second heap of combustibles. The wagon hung half over the ragged edge of the floor.

"It should take about fifteen minutes for the fire to burn through the rope," Brett said. "Then the wagon will fall and dump the hot coals in the gasoline. By then it will have spread all over the surface and flowed down side tunnels into other parts of the cavern system."

"But it may not get them all."

"It will get some of them. It's the best we can do right now. You get the fire going in the wagon; I'll start this one up."

Dhuva sniffed the air. "That fluid," he said. "We know it in Wavly as phlogistoneum. The wealthy use it for cooking."

"We'll use it to cook Gels." Brett struck a match. The fire leaped up, smoking. Dhuva watched, struck his match awkwardly, started his blaze. They stood for a moment watching. The nylon curled and blackened, melting in the heat.

"We'd better get moving," Brett said. "It doesn't look as though it will last fifteen minutes."

They stepped out into the street. Behind them wisps of smoke curled from the door. Dhuva seized Brett's arm. "Look!"

Half a block away the fat man in the panama hat strode toward them at the head of a group of men in grey flannel. "That's him!" the fat man shouted, "the one I told you about. I knew the scoundrel would be back!" He slowed, eyeing Brett and Dhuva warily.

"You'd better get away from here, fast!" Brett called. "There'll be an explosion in a few minutes —"

"Smoke!" the fat man yelped. "Fire! They've set fire to the city! There it is! pouring out of the window . . . and the door!" He started forward. Brett yanked the pistol from the holster, thumbed back the hammer.

"Stop right there!" he barked. "For your own good I'm telling you to run. I don't care about that crowd of golems you've collected, but I'd hate to see a real human get hurt — even a cowardly one like you."

"These are honest citizens," the fat man gasped, standing, staring at the gun. "You won't get away with this. We all know you. You'll be dealt with . . ."

"We're going now. And you're going too."

"You can't kill us all," the fat man said. He licked his lips. "We won't let you destroy our city."

As the fat man turned to exhort his followers Brett fired, once twice, three times. Three golems fell on their faces. The fat man whirled.

"Devil!" he shrieked. "A killer is abroad!" He charged, mouth open. Brett ducked aside, tripped the fat man. He fell heavily, slamming his face against the pavement. The golems surged forward. Brett and Dhuva slammed punches to the sternum, took clumsy blows on the shoulder, back, chest. Golems fell. Brett ducked a wild swing, toppled his attacker, turned to see Dhuva deal with the last of the dummies. The fat man sat in the street, dabbing at his bleeding nose, the panama still in place.

"Get up," Brett commanded. "There's no time left."

"You've killed them. Killed them all . . ." The fat man got to his feet, then turned suddenly and plunged for the door from which a cloud of smoke poured. Brett hauled him back. He and Dhuva started off, dragging the struggling man between them. They had gone a block when their prisoner, with a sudden frantic jerk, freed himself, set off at a run for the fire.

"Let him go!" Dhuva cried. "It's too late to go back!"

The fat man leaped fallen golems, wrestled with the door, disappeared into the smoke. Brett and Dhuva sprinted for the corner. As they rounded it a tremendous blast shook the street. The pavement before them quivered, opened in a wide crack. A ten-foot section dropped from view. They skirted the gaping hole, dashed for safety as the façades along the street cracked, fell in clouds of dust. The street trembled under a second explosion. Cracks opened, dust rising in puffs from the long wavering lines. Masonry collapsed around them. They put their heads down and ran.

*W*inded, Brett and Dhuva walked through the empty streets of the city. Behind them, smoke blackened the sky. Embers floated down around them. The odor of burning Gel was carried on the wind. The late sun shone on the blank pavement. A lone golem in a tasseled fez, left over from the morning's parade, leaned stiffly against a lamp post, eyes blank. Empty cars sat in driveways. TV antennae stood forlornly against the sunset.

"That place looks lived-in," said Brett, indicating an open apartment window with a curtain billowing above a potted geranium. "I'll take a look."

He came back shaking his head. "They were all in the TV room. They looked so natural at first; I mean, they didn't look up or anything when I walked in. I turned the set off. The electricity is still working anyway. Wonder how long it will last?"

They turned down a residential street. Underfoot the pavement trembled at a distant blast. They skirted a crack, kept going. Occasional golems stood in awkward poses or lay across sidewalks. One, clad in black, tilted awkwardly in a gothic entry of fretted stone work. "I guess there won't be any church this Sunday," said Brett.

He halted before a brown brick apartment house. An untended hose welled on a patch of sickly lawn. Brett went to the door, stood listening, then went in. Across the room the still figure of a woman sat in a rocker. A curl stirred on her smooth forehead. A flicker of expression seemed to cross the lined face. Brett started forward. "Don't be afraid. You can come with us —"

He stopped. A flapping window-shade cast restless shadows on the still golem features on which dust was already settling. Brett turned away, shaking his head.

"All of them," he said. "It's as though they were snipped out of paper. When the Gels died their dummies died with them."

"Why?" said Dhuva. "What does it all mean?"

"Mean?" said Brett. He shook his head, started off again along the street. "It doesn't mean anything. It's just the way things are."

*B*rett sat in a deserted Cadillac, tuning the radio.

". . . anybody hear me?" said a plaintive voice from the speaker. "This is Ab Gullorian, at the Twin Spires. Looks like I'm the only one left alive. Can anybody hear me?"

Brett tuned. ". . . been asking the wrong questions . . . looking for the Final Fact. Now these are strange matters, brothers. But if a flower blooms, what man shall ask why? What lore do we seek in a symphony. . . ?"

He twisted the knob again. ". . . Kansas City. Not more than half a dozen of us. And the dead! Piled all over the place. But it's a funny thing: Doc Potter started to do an autopsy —"

Brett turned the knob. ". . . CQ, CQ, CQ. This is Hollip Quate, calling CQ, CQ. There's been a disaster here at Port Wanderlust. We need —"

"Take Jesus into your hearts," another station urged.

". . . to base," the radio said faintly, with much crackling. "Lunar Observatory to base. Come in, Lunar

Control. This is Commander McVee of the Lunar Detachment, sole survivor —"

". . . hello, Hollip Quate? Hollip Quate? This is Kansas City calling. Say, where did you say you were calling from. . . ?"

"It looks as though both of us had a lot of mistaken ideas about the world outside," said Brett. "Most of these stations sound as though they might as well be coming from Mars."

"I don't understand where the voices come from," Dhuva said. "But all the places they name are strange to me . . . except the Twin Spires."

"I've heard of Kansas City," Brett said, "but none of the other ones."

The ground trembled. A low rumble rolled. "Another one," Brett said. He switched off the radio, tried the starter. It groaned, turned over. The engine caught, sputtered, then ran smoothly.

"Get in, Dhuva. We might as well ride. Which way do we go to get out of this place?"

"The wall lies in that direction," said Dhuva. "But I don't know about a gate."

"We'll worry about that when we get to it," said Brett. "This whole place is going to collapse before long. We really started something. I suppose other underground storage tanks caught — and gas lines, too."

A building ahead cracked, fell in a heap of pulverized plaster. The car bucked as a blast sent a ripple down the street. A manhole cover popped up, clattered a few feet, dropped from sight. Brett swerved, gunned the car. It leaped over rubble, roared along the littered pavement. Brett looked in the rear-view mirror. A block behind them the street ended. Smoke and dust rose from the immense pit.

"We just missed it that time!" he called. "How far to the wall?"

"Not far! Turn here . . ."

Brett rounded the corner with a shrieking of tires. Ahead the grey wall rose up, blank, featureless.

"This is a dead end!" Brett shouted.

"We'd better get out and run for it —"

"No time! I'm going to ram the wall! Maybe I can knock a hole in it."

*D*huva crouched; teeth gritted, Brett held the accelerator to the floor, roared straight toward the wall. The heavy car shot across the last few yards, struck —

And burst through a curtain of canvas into a field of dry stalks.

Brett steered the car in a wide curve to halt and look back. A blackened panama hat floated down, settled among the stalks. Smoke poured up in a dense cloud from behind the canvas wall. A fetid stench pervaded the air.

"That finishes that, I guess," Brett said.

"I don't know. Look there."

Brett turned. Far across the dry field columns of smoke rose from the ground.

"The whole thing's undermined," Brett said. "How far does it go?"

"No telling. But we'd better be off. Perhaps we can get beyond the edge of it. Not that it matters. We're all that's left . . ."

"You sound like the fat man," Brett said. "But why should we be so surprised to find out the truth? After all, we never saw it before. All we knew — or thought we knew — was what they told us. The moon, the other side of the world, a distant city . . . or even the next town. How do we really know what's there . . . unless we go and see for ourselves? Does a goldfish in his bowl know what the ocean is like?"

"Where did they come from, those Gels? How much of the world have they undermined? What about Wavly? Is it a golem country too? The Duke . . . and all the people I knew?"

"I don't know, Dhuva. I've been wondering about the people in Casperton. Like Doc Welch. I used to see him in the street with his little black bag. I always thought it was full of pills and scalpels; but maybe it really had zebra's tails and toad's eyes in it. Maybe he's really a magician on his way to cast spells against demons. Maybe the people I used to see hurrying to catch the bus every morning weren't really going to the office. Maybe they go down into caves and chip away at the foundations of things. Maybe they go up on rooftops and put on rainbow-colored robes and fly away. I used to pass by a bank in Casperton: a big grey stone building with little curtains over the bottom half of the windows. I never go in there. I don't have anything to do in a bank. I've always thought it was full of bankers, banking . . . Now I don't know. It could be anything . . ."

"That's why I'm afraid," Dhuva said. "It could be anything."

"Things aren't really any different than they were," said Brett, ". . . except that now we know." He turned the big car out across the field toward Casperton.

"I don't know what we'll find when we get back. Aunt Haicey, Pretty-Lee . . . But there's only one way to find out."

The moon rose as the car bumped westward, raising a trail of dust against the luminous sky of evening.

THE END